To all those who want to be
hippie grandmothers – including me!
R. L.

To my mum and dad
A. C.

First published 2003 by Walker Books Ltd
87 Vauxhall Walk, London SE11 5HJ

2 4 6 8 10 9 7 5 3 1

Text © 2003 Reeve Lindbergh
Illustrations © 2003 Abby Carter

The right of Reeve Lindbergh and Abby Carter to be identified as author and illustrator
respectively of this work has been asserted by them in accordance with the
Copyright, Designs and Patents Act 1988

This book has been typeset in Tapioca

Printed in Italy

British Library Cataloguing in Publication Data:
a catalogue record for this book
is available from the British Library

ISBN 0-7445-5658-9

My Hippie Grandmother

written by
Reeve Lindbergh

illustrated by
Abby Carter

WALKER BOOKS
AND SUBSIDIARIES
LONDON • BOSTON • SYDNEY

I have a hippie grandmother.
I'm really glad she's mine.
She hasn't cut her hair at all
Since nineteen sixty-nine.

I live in town on Tinworth Street
With Mum and Dad and Russ,
But Grandma lives behind the hill
And drives a purple bus.

She has a cat called Woodstock,
A fish named Tiny Tim
And a boyfriend with a big moustache.
(Her boyfriend's name is Jim.)

She has plants on every windowsill.
Green vines grow in the shower.
There are posters in her bedroom.
They say LOVE and FLOWER POWER!

I help her in her garden.
We hoe the peas and beans.
We eat sunflower-and-honey bread
In bare feet and ripped jeans.

We're at the Farmer's Market
By noon each Saturday.
We sell some bread and vegetables,
And some we give away.

Granny's JAMS

Sometimes I go with Grandma
To picket the town hall.
If no one passes by, she says,
"Oh well, can't win 'em all!"

At night she pulls her banjo out
And Jim gets his guitar.
We sing the song "Amazing Grace"
And wish upon a star.

The moon shines at the window.
The cat purrs by my feet.
I curl up warm and fall asleep
On a psychedelic sheet.

My mother is a teacher.
My dad works on TV.
My grandma says someday I'll find
The perfect job for me.

I might become Prime Minister
Or go to outer space,
Or find a cure for cancer
And save the human race.

I tell her there's one other thing
I really want to do:
"Become a Hippie Grandmother,
So I can be LIKE YOU!"